Secret Kingdom

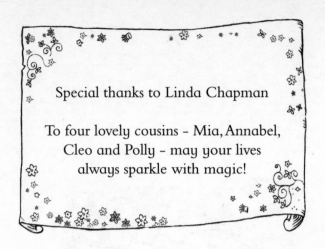

Special thanks to Linda Chapman

To four lovely cousins – Mia, Annabel,
Cleo and Polly – may your lives
always sparkle with magic!

ORCHARD BOOKS
338 Euston Road, London NW1 3BH
Orchard Books Australia
Level 17/207 Kent Street, Sydney, NSW 2000
A Paperback Original

First published in 2013 by Orchard Books

A CIP catalogue record for this book is available
from the British Library.

ISBN 978 1 40832 340 3

1 3 5 7 9 10 8 6 4 2

Printed in Great Britain

The paper and board used in this paperback are natural recyclable
products made from wood grown in sustainable forests. The
manufacturing processes conform to the environmental regulations
of the country of origin.

Orchard Books is a division of Hachette Children's Books,
an Hachette UK company

www.hachette.co.uk

Series created by Hothouse Fiction
www.hothousefiction.com

Snow Bear Sanctuary

ROSIE BANKS

ORCHARD

This is the Secret Kingdom

Contents

At the Zoo

The leopard cub pounced on a fallen leaf and rolled onto its back.

"Oh, isn't he cute!" Summer Hammond squealed as the cub wrestled with the leaf and yowled at the people watching from outside his enclosure at Honeyvale Zoo. "I wish I could cuddle him," Summer said longingly as she turned to her two best friends, Ellie Macdonald and Jasmine Smith.

"Just like you wanted to cuddle the wombat we saw, and the chipmunks and the baby elephant," laughed Jasmine.

"I think you'd even cuddle a stick insect if you could, Summer!" teased Ellie.

Summer grinned. "Yep, but the leopard cub is definitely my favourite."

She looked at the cub, who was now wobbling his way along a branch. "I'm so glad your mum and grandma decided to take us to the zoo today, Jasmine."

"Me too." Ellie grinned. It was a bright, crisp autumn day, perfect for visiting the zoo! "There are so many amazing animals and birds here. I like the parrots best," she added, thinking of the brightly-coloured birds they'd seen swooping round a big aviary earlier. "They were such beautiful colours. I'd love to paint them."

"I like the orang-utans," said Jasmine. She jumped up and down, her dark hair bouncing on her shoulders. "OO-OO-OO! I'd like to be like an orang-utan and make lots of noise!"

"You already do!" grinned Ellie.

Jasmine giggled.

"Where should we go next?" Summer asked.

"There's a map over there," Jasmine pointed out. They all ran over to a big board showing a map of the whole zoo. It was covered with colourful pictures of the elephant, zebra and giraffe enclosures, the penguin pool, the monkey cages and the houses where the snakes, bats and insects lived.

"This reminds me of another map," Jasmine said. She dropped her voice to a whisper. "The map of the Secret Kingdom!"

The girls exchanged smiles. They shared an incredible secret. Ever since they'd found a magical box at their school jumble sale, they'd been on lots

of amazing adventures in an enchanted
land called the Secret Kingdom.

"I wonder when we'll get another
message from the Secret Kingdom," said
Summer.

"I bet it won't be long," replied
Jasmine. "Not with four fairytale baddies
still on the loose!"

Evil Queen Malice was always trying
to cause problems in the kingdom
because she wanted to rule instead of
her brother, the kindly King Merry. Her
latest wicked plan had been to release
six baddies from a book of fairytales into
the kingdom. She hoped that they would
cause so much trouble that the people
would beg her to rule just to make them
stop. So far the girls had managed to put
a giant and a wicked witch back into the

book but there were still four more scary fairytale characters to find.

"I wonder who we'll have to stop next," said Ellie.

"And how fierce they'll be," added Summer, playing nervously with the end of one of her long blonde pigtails. The giant and witch had both been horrible!

"We'd better be ready to go at any time," said Jasmine. "Maybe we should check the Magic Box. It might have a message for us."

Summer took her bag off her back. She had brought the box with her just in case their friends in the Secret Kingdom tried to send them a message. But just as she started to open the top of her bag, she heard Mrs Smith, Jasmine's mum, calling to them.

"Yoo-hoo, girls! Over here!" Jasmine's mum was coming out of the nearby café where she had been having a cup of tea with Jasmine's grandma.

"We'll look at the box later," Jasmine whispered.

"Shall we go and see the penguins now?" suggested Mrs Smith.

The girls nodded eagerly. They all loved the penguins with their funny waddling walks and their twinkly black eyes. They set off with Jasmine's mum and grandma. As they neared the penguin pool, Summer hung back a little. She wanted to check the Magic Box just in case there was a message from their friends.

She opened the top of her bag excitedly, just in time to see a spark of light flash across the mirror, followed by another and another.

Suddenly the mirror glowed with a bright light!

Summer gave a squeak of surprise and hastily shut the bag so no one could see. She had to tell the others!

She rushed over to where Jasmine and Ellie were staring down into the penguin pool. Mrs Smith was looking at the information board to see what time the penguins were being fed and Jasmine's grandma was chatting to another family who were also watching the penguins.

"Jasmine! Ellie!" Summer whispered. "The Magic Box is glowing!"

"Oh, wow!" Ellie hissed. "Is there a message?"

"I didn't see. I couldn't look for long."

Jasmine glanced round. "Let's go over there where it's quiet."

She led the way over to another sign. It was big enough for them to stand behind without being seen. The girls ducked behind it and Summer opened her bag again. Sparkling light spilled out. Excitement rushed through the girls as they saw words forming in the mirrored

lid. It was the riddle that would whisk them away! They were having a great time at the zoo, but going to the Secret Kingdom would be even better!

Off On Another Adventure

Summer read the riddle out:

*"On frosty slopes where snowflakes fall,
Find a shelter for snow bears small."*

The lid of the box sprang open and
the magic map floated out. It hovered
in the air for a moment and then floated
down to the grass, opening itself out as
it settled there. The girls crowded round

it. Through the map they could see down into the kingdom where unicorns galloped through grassy meadows, mermaids waved from the sea and gold flags were flying from the turrets of the Enchanted Palace.

Summer bit her lip. If they were needed, there must be trouble somewhere in the kingdom – but where? Her eyes ran over some of the places she had visited – Bubble Volcano, Dream Dale, Sugarsweet Bakery...

"The riddle says we need to look for somewhere cold," said Jasmine.

"Magic Mountain is very cold," said Ellie, pointing to the slopes of a high mountain, covering in pink snow. They'd been there once before and met some friendly snow brownies who had been very cold when Queen Malice had made their Everwarm Embers go out.

"It looks very quiet on the frosty slopes," said Summer. Usually there were lots of brownies skiing, but today the mountain was empty.

Jasmine peered closer. "Look at that little house on the mountainside. I've never noticed it before."

She pointed at a cosy-looking higgledy-piggledy log cabin with smoke puffing out of its chimney. It was on the edge of a forest of pine trees that covered part of the upper slopes of the mountain. Next to it was a tiny label. "Snow Bear Sanctuary," Jasmine read out.

"I bet that's where we've got to go!" exclaimed Ellie.

"Of course! A sanctuary is another

name for a shelter!" said Summer. "Let's try!" She loved the thought of going to a shelter for snow bears – maybe they'd be like polar bears... Summer liked to think she knew a lot about all kinds of animals, but she'd never heard of a snow bear before!

The girls quickly put their hands on the six gems that surrounded the mirror and called out: "Snow Bear Sanctuary!"

There was a bright silver flash and suddenly a sparkling light zoomed in front of them, zipping this way and that.

"Trixi!" cried the girls. Their friend Trixi, the tiny royal pixie, came to rest on the grass. She was standing on the magic leaf she used for whizzing about.

"Hello, girls!" she cried. "I'm glad you got my message. We need your help as quickly as possible!"

Trixi looked
dressed for the cold,
wearing a fur-
trimmed cape,
green woolly
tights and bright
red snow boots.
Her blonde hair
was covered with
a fluffy white hat.

"What's
happening?" asked
Ellie.

"There's something odd going on at
Snow Bear Sanctuary. We think one of
Queen Malice's fairytale baddies might
be causing trouble nearby."

"Then what are we waiting for?" asked

Jasmine, glad that no time passed in the human world when they visited the Secret Kingdom. Her mum and grandma wouldn't miss them at all while they went on an adventure. "Let's go!"

The girls grabbed hands and Trixi tapped the green ring on her finger, calling out a spell as she did so:

"Magic ring, whisk us away
To where the snow bears live and play!"

The girls felt themselves spinning round in a cloud of sparkling light. Faster and faster they spun until the lights around them cleared and they found themselves in a clear blue sky, floating down towards the ground in a cloud of soft snowflakes.

"Yikes!" gulped Ellie, who was scared of heights. She shut her eyes tight and gripped Summer and Jasmine's hands.

"Don't worry. The magic will keep you safe and we'll be down soon," said Trixi soothingly, dodging the snowflakes on her leaf.

"Oh, wow!" gasped Jasmine as she saw the slopes of Magic Mountain below them. Fresh pink snow stretched out like a thick blanket and the pine trees' branches were weighed down with sparkling icicles. Her hand reached up to her dark hair. She and Summer and Ellie were all wearing the special tiaras that always appeared when they were in the Secret Kingdom. When they wore them everyone knew they were Very Important Friends of King Merry's!

Jasmine realised Trixi's magic had changed their clothes too. Thick gloves and scarves had appeared, and they were all wearing cosy boots. Ellie's were red with pom-poms, Jasmine's were tan with fake fur and toggles, and Summer's were covered with a pretty pink pattern.

"Look at what we're wearing!" said
Jasmine as they twirled round.

Ellie kept her eyes squeezed shut. "No
thanks!"

"Don't worry, Ellie. We're almost
down," said Summer.

"Here we go!" said Jasmine, seeing the
snowy ground approaching.

The magic dropped them into a deep snowdrift. They all sat up and shook the pink snow crystals from their coats and hair.

"Oh, wow," Ellie said, finally opening her eyes and taking in the beautiful snowy landscape and dark pine trees nearby. "I'd forgotten how beautiful Magic Mountain is. I wish I could draw it."

"Where's Snow Bear Sanctuary?" Summer asked eagerly.

"Just over here!" Trixi hovered in front

of them on her leaf and pointed up the hill. "Follow me!"

The girls struggled out of the soft snow and looked up at the large wood cabin they had seen on the map. Its lights were on and it was surrounded by three smaller buildings also made out of wood. There was a well-trodden pathway going between each hut and the main house, and pretty bushes covered with red berries were scattered in front of the cabin. Smoke puffed from its little chimney and as they started to walk closer, Summer could see little lacy curtains at the window and a red doormat.

"Winterberry!" Trixi called as she whizzed on ahead. "Are you there? It's me – Trixi!"

For a moment there was no reply, and then the door of one of the outbuildings opened and an old brownie came hurrying out. Her bright-pink skin was wrinkled but her purple eyes were bright. Like all snow brownies she had pointed ears and was roughly half the size of the girls. She gave them a beaming smile as her eyes took in the girls' tiaras. "Trixi, how lovely to see you! And King Merry's honoured friends from the Other Realm! Oh, I am glad you're here. Something very strange is going on. My name is Winterberry," she said.

"Hi, I'm Jasmine and this is Ellie and Summer," said Jasmine. "We'll try our best to help you if we can."

"Is this really a snow bear sanctuary?" said Summer, her eagerness to see the bears overcoming her usual shyness.

Winterberry beamed. "It certainly is!"

"Winterberry has been looking after the bears all her life," said Trixi.

"My mother looked after them before me and before her my grandmother did," said Winterberry. "The bears usually spend their time in the forest but they need somewhere to come if they get too cold or hungry or ill. I look after them until they are ready to go back to the forest."

"So, what's been happening?" asked Ellie, rubbing her hands in the cold.

"Why do you need our help?"

"Come inside and I'll tell you all about it," said Winterberry. "I've got a fire burning and it won't take me any time at all to rustle up some hot chocolate and cookies. Does that sound good?"

"Oh, yes!" chorused the girls in delight. Hot chocolate and cookies always sounded good!

They followed Winterberry into the pine cabin. Inside the front door there was a small hallway that led to different rooms. Winterberry pushed open an old oak door into a lounge with a cosy old sofa, three armchairs and a fire burning in the grate. A multi-coloured rug covered the wooden floorboards. As soon as the girls walked in they gasped.

Two baby bears with fluffy, light-pink fur were curled up on the sofa and a third was stretched out on the rug in front of the fire. They were all snoring gently, their ears flickering and their paws twitching as they dreamed.

"Meet my snow bear cubs," said Winterberry with a smile.

❧Snow Bears!

Just then, the snow bear cub on the rug woke up. He had bright black eyes and looked just like a baby polar bear, only his thick, fluffy fur was pale pink. He put his head on one side and made a soft rumbling noise in his throat.

"Oh, he's gorgeous!" breathed Summer in delight.

The cub padded over to her, his tiny

paws slipping slightly on the wooden
floorboards as he left the rug.

"Snow bears are very friendly," said
Winterberry as the other cubs woke up
too and looked at the girls with interest.
"You can say hello to them."

Summer kneeled down and stroked the
cub by her feet while
Jasmine and Ellie
went over to
the sofa and
stroked the
two babies
there. The cub
climbed upon
to Summer's
knees. He was
soft and warm
and she couldn't

resist giving him a hug. "You're so beautiful," she told him, stroking his soft fur. He made a contented purring noise and nuzzled her face with his black nose.

"There are lots more bears in the house – and in the sheds outside," said Winterberry.

As she spoke, another bear stood up from behind the sofa. This one looked like a grown-up bear, but it was still only as tall as Summer.

"Usually only the baby bears stay in the house," Winterberry explained, "but so many bears have come to stay that there's not enough room for them in the shelters outside."

Another two bears poked their noses out from behind the armchairs. A fourth bear came padding in from the hallway

to say hello. The girls didn't have
enough hands to stroke them all!

"I'll go and get us something to eat and
drink!" said Winterberry, squeezing past
the bears and hurrying into the kitchen.

"Aren't snow bears gorgeous?" said
Ellie, stroking one of the older bears. His
fur was thicker and slightly coarser than
the fluffy baby cubs. He snuffled at her
cheek and made a deep rumbling noise
in his throat.

"They're so cute!" agreed Summer as the cub she was playing with rolled over onto his back, waving his little paws in the air.

Jasmine leaned over to tickle his tummy. "You're adorable!" One of the adult bears snuffled at her neck. She giggled and squirmed. "Okay, you're all adorable!"

"Here we are, everyone," said Winterberry, carrying in a tray with hot chocolate in mugs, a plate of chocolate chip cookies, a huge jar of jam and three large baby bottles. "It's almost time for the cubs' next feed," she went on. "Would you like to help me once you've had something to eat and drink?"

"Oh, yes please!" chorused all three girls excitedly.

Winterberry handed out the cookies and hot chocolate. She had even filled a tiny mug for Trixi. The hot chocolate was delicious — it tasted like it was made from real melted chocolate and had marshmallows floating on top. The cookies were freshly baked and still warm from the oven. The snow bear cubs sniffed at them eagerly.

"Don't let them have any," warned Trixi. "Snow bear cubs are very greedy but they should only really drink milk and eat jam when they're babies."

"Jam?" echoed Summer. She'd never heard of baby animals eating jam before!

"Oh, yes," said Trixi nodding. "It's a special type of jam — bearberry jam. Snow bears really love it. It's very good for them too."

When the girls had finished their hot chocolate, Winterberry handed each of them a bottle of milk and a spoon, then she took the lid off the big jar of dark-pink jam that was on the tray. "Here we are!" she said cheerfully. "This is all you need to do!"

She gently pushed the older bears out of the way and scooped up one of the cubs from the sofa. Rolling him onto his back, she held him like a baby and let him suck at the bottle. Every so often he would stop drinking and she fed him a spoonful of bearberry jam from the jar. "It's easy," she said. She handed the bear to Ellie. Jasmine and Summer picked up the other two cubs. They were so soft and warm! The bears snuggled into the crooks of the girls' arms. Picking up the bottles, the girls started to feed the cubs. They sucked contentedly at the milk. Summer sighed happily as her bear wriggled contentedly in her arms. She was in heaven!

Winterberry smiled. "This is so much easier with you girls to help. It usually takes ages to feed the three cubs, and then there are all the other bears too,"

she said affectionately, stroking the two older bears nearest to her. "I'm busy from dawn till dusk, feeding them and cleaning out the shelters, and this week there seem to be more bears than ever before! Soon I'm going to be completely overrun! I don't know how I'm going to cope. I've never known so many bears need my help."

"We can help you with them while we're here," said Summer eagerly. She couldn't think of anything she would like more than to help look after lots of snow bears.

"Definitely!" said Ellie.

Jasmine nodded. "So why are there so many snow bears here at the moment?"

"That's what I'm hoping you can help me find out!" said Winterberry.

"Something isn't right in the forest. The bears all seem really scared. A few days ago I found some very strange footprints in the forest, and this morning there were some right outside the cabin! I've never seen anything like them."

"What did they look like?" asked Trixi curiously.

"As soon as the cubs have finished I'll show you," said Winterberry.

When the cubs had drained their bottles they all sighed sleepily. The girls put them down on the sofa. Summer grinned as the cubs cuddled up in a heap and shut their eyes.

Soon they could hear the cubs snoring softly.

"Come with me," Winterberry whispered. They all went back out into the frosty sunshine with Trixi flying beside them. Winterberry led the way through the snow to the edge of the forest. Just inside the first row of trees, she pointed down at the ground. There was a massive footprint about three times as big as one of Summer's feet with four round toe marks. "Look at that!" the brownie said.

"Oh, no!" cried Summer, her face going pale.

They all looked at her. "What is it, Summer?" said Jasmine. "Do you know what makes footprints like that?"

Summer gasped. "I think so. I'm sure I

remember there being a creature in my fairytale book that might make footprints like that – an ogre!" She shivered as she spoke the word.

"An ogre?" Ellie echoed.

"That's not good," said Winterberry, looking worried. "Not good at all. Aren't ogres supposed to be very greedy? I've heard they eat everything they see – no wonder the snow bears are scared of being in the forest if there's a great big ogre on the loose!"

"Well, if there is, we'll catch it and put it back in the fairytale book," said Jasmine, determinedly. "We're not going to stand by and watch the bears being scared away from their home."

"No way!" said Summer.

"Oh, thank you," said Winterberry,

clasping her hands together gratefully.

"Have you got the fairytale book, Trixi?" Ellie asked. They'd need it to get rid of the ogre.

"Here it is!" Trixi pulled a tiny book out from her pocket. "I shrank it down to my size so I could keep it safe."

"So, I guess now we just need to find the ogre," said Jasmine.

Summer thought about the bear cubs curled up on the sofa. "Let's hurry!" she said. "We have to make the forest safe · for the bears again!"

Following the Footprints

"We must be very careful," warned Trixi. "From the size of these footprints, the ogre must be huge!"

Winterberry shuddered. "Are you sure we should go?"

"You don't need to come," Summer said to the little brownie. "Won't the bears need you here?"

"Yes," said Winterberry with a sigh.

"They'll all be wanting their lunch soon and the ones in the sheds will need fresh water and bedding too." She ran a hand through her grey hair. "I don't know how I'm going to do it all."

"Why don't we give you a hand before we set off?" suggested Jasmine, seeing how tired the old brownie looked. "The ogre will still be in the forest when we've finished helping you and we can try and track him down then."

"Well, that would be wonderful. Thank you," said Winterberry. "You know the old saying… 'Many brownies make cake quickly!'"

Ellie smiled. "Actually we don't. In our world we say 'Many hands make light work.' But I think I like the Secret Kingdom saying better!"

So the girls and Trixi set about helping
Winterberry. Each of the outside shelters
had four cosy stalls filled with thick
beds of golden straw and big feed and
water bowls. There were snow bears
of all shapes and sizes, from grown-up
bears that were as tall as the girls, to
young bears who were about the size
of a Labrador dog. They were all very
friendly and greeted the girls with deep
rumbling noises.

The girls set about cleaning out the stalls, pushing wheelbarrows full of fresh straw, filling up water troughs and then handing out big buckets of bearberries mixed with sweet-smelling hay – the bears' favourite food.

When all the bears were happy and fed, the girls set off into the forest following the trail of footprints that led through the trees. Trixi flew beside them on her leaf. The sun was shining in the blue sky and the snow glittered as if it was coated with tiny diamonds. As the girls walked down the path they breathed in the cold air, which was scented with pine needles. It was very still and silent in the trees. There were no birds singing and no animals running amongst the branches.

Summer looked round, her heart beating a little faster as her feet crunched on the snow and they went deeper into the forest. What if there was a terrifying ogre with big teeth just ahead? What if it was watching them from the trees?

CRASH!

They all jumped as they heard a loud noise in the trees behind them. Summer squeaked in alarm.

CRASH! SNAP! Something was definitely approaching. Something very noisy!

"It's the ogre!" hissed Ellie.

"Help!" cried Trixi.

Summer felt like her heart was going to jump out of her throat.

Jasmine grabbed a broken branch from the floor. "Who's there?" she shouted bravely, brandishing the branch. "Stop where you are!"

Summer and Ellie grabbed branches too.

The crashing grew louder. The girls tensed and then, suddenly, the three fluffy snow bear cubs bounded out of the trees, their little dark eyes shining as they gambolled towards the girls.

"It's only the baby snow bears!" cried Ellie. "It's not the ogre after all!"

The cubs leaped at the girls, licking them in delight.

"They must have followed us!" said Summer, giggling in relief. "Oh, you naughty cubs. You gave us such a scare!"

"I really thought the ogre was coming to get us!" said Jasmine, crouching down to stroke the happy bears.

One of the cubs put his paws up on Summer's leg and she ruffled his fur. "Winterberry's going to be wondering where you are," she scolded gently.

"We'd better take them back," said Ellie.

Summer nodded and bent down to pick the nearest cub up but he scampered away through the trees, following the ogre's footprints.

"No, don't go that way! Come back!" Jasmine cried in alarm. But it was too late! The other two cubs were charging after him.

The girls and Trixi ran after them. "Stop!" cried Ellie. "Please, wait!"

But the cubs looked over their shoulders and seemed to think the girls just wanted to play chase. They sped up, their four legs making them much faster than the girls.

"What if they meet the ogre?" gasped Ellie.

"Trixi, can you do anything to stop them?" Summer panted.

"I can try a spell!" Trixi said as she zoomed along. "Let me think...Yes, I know!" she cried. She tapped her ring.

"Bearberry jam, in a bowl big and round,
A treat for bears, on snowy ground!"

A bright green flash lit up the path in front of the bears and suddenly a big bowl of bearberry jam appeared! The cubs skidded to a halt, their black eyes wide in surprise. Their noses twitched. They forgot all about running away and bounded up to the jam. They started to eat it with happy growls and snuffles.

"Brilliant, Trixi!" said Summer. She and the others ran up to the cubs and

scooped them up as the bears licked the last of the jam out of the bowl. The fur around their noses was even pinker than usual and very sticky.

"Now you're definitely going home!" said Jasmine firmly as Trixi tapped her pixie ring again and made the bowl disappear.

"Come on," said Summer, turning round. "We'll carry you."

"Shh!" Ellie hissed suddenly. "Listen. What's that noise?"

They all fell quiet. There was a noise coming from further on through the trees. It sounded like voices arguing.

"That's not an ogre," whispered Trixi.

"So who is it?" said Jasmine. She glanced nervously at the others. "Shall we go and see?"

They nodded. Clutching the bears
tightly, they crept towards the noise.

As they reached the point where the broken branches ended they stopped and stared. Just in front of them, standing next to a frozen pond, five Storm Sprites were crouching down, making ogre footprints in the snow!

The Wicked Plan

The Storm Sprites were Queen Malice's horrible helpers. Their skin was grey and they had leathery bat-like wings and mean little eyes. One of them was pressing a large wooden stamp into the snow. When the Storm Sprite pulled the stamp up, it left the perfect footprint of an ogre!

"You're not doing it right, slug-brain!" jeered one of the others. "That looks like the footprint of a giant mouse!"

"You couldn't do it better, cabbage ears!" retorted the Storm Sprite with the stamp.

"I could so!"

"Couldn't!"

"Could!"

"What does it matter?" cackled another. "They're good enough to fool those silly girls. They think we're the ogre."

"Yes, those girls are as brainless as beetles!" agreed another.

Jasmine swung round to the others. "I can't believe it! Those footprints weren't real – the Storm Sprites have been tricking us!" she hissed furiously. "Well, not any more!"

"What are you going to do?" said Ellie worriedly.

In answer, Jasmine marched out into the clearing. "Stop right there, you silly sprites!" she cried angrily. The sprites were so surprised they jumped in fright, and the one with the stamp fell over onto his bottom.

"What do you think you're doing?" Jasmine demanded, hands on her hips.

The spites quickly recovered. "Tricking you!" one of them cackled. "We knew you'd follow the footprints away from that silly bear sanctuary. You're so stupid and we're so clever!"

"So, there isn't an ogre?" asked Summer, coming forward, still clutching one of the snow bears.

"Oh, there's an ogre all right!" said the Storm Sprite, nodding. "A very big scary

one. But he didn't leave the footprints you've been following."

"So, where is the ogre?" demanded Jasmine.

"Aha!" The sprite looked shifty. "That would be telling!"

"I can't believe you tricked us!" said Trixi, shaking her head.

"*Why* did you trick us?" said Ellie. Storm Sprites were annoying, mean creatures but why had they gone to the trouble of leading the girls away from Snow Bear Sanctuary? It seemed a very strange thing to do.

The Storm Sprite looked at the others, who nodded. "Well, we did it because—" But his words were cut off by a shriek of harsh laughter. It seemed to be coming from the frozen pond!

"Look!" cried Summer as a spark of light ran across the pond's icy surface.

The girls and Trixi stared as an image of Queen Malice's face appeared in the ice. Her frizzy black hair was sticking out around her head, her dark eyes glittering with triumph. "They did it because I told them to, you foolish children! I didn't want you near that cabin, spoiling my fun."

"What fun?" A chill stole over Jasmine as she looked into the queen's cruel face. What had she got planned now?

"The fun I'm going to have as the

ogre destroys the snow bears' precious sanctuary! Watch and see what's happening back with your silly brownie friend right now." Queen Malice screamed in delight and the picture changed. Her face faded and was replaced by a picture of Winterberry's cabin and the other wooden huts. A massive ogre was stomping towards the cabin door. He had a big club in his hands and green warty skin. His long, sharp teeth were sticking out from his mouth and he had two bumpy horns on his forehead. He was wearing raggedy clothes and had a hungry expression on his ugly face. He opened his mouth and bellowed loudly.

"No!" gasped Summer as he lifted his club and swung it at the door.

They saw the
wooden door
start to splinter.
He raised the
club and took
aim again.

Queen Malice's
shrieking laughter
rang out and the
picture faded as her face came back into
view. "That's why my sprites led you out
here!" she cackled.

"We'll go back!" Jasmine said bravely,
her heart pounding. If they ran as fast as
they could, maybe they could get back
to help Winterberry before the ogre did
too much damage. She only hoped the
elderly brownie would stay out of his way
and not try to tackle him on her own.

"We'll trap him in the book!" Ellie said defiantly.

"Oh, will you?" sneered the queen. "Well, first you'll have to find your way back and that isn't going to be easy!" Her eyes gleamed and she called out a spell.

**"Trees twist, paths move on the ground
So the way back cannot be found!"**

All around the girls, the trees suddenly started to move and twist into new shapes. The path they had come down disappeared behind them.

"You'll never find your way back in time now. Never!" shrieked the queen.

There was a bright flash and her face disappeared from the frozen lake.

The Storm Sprites cackled with laughter. "You heard Queen Malice!" one of them taunted. "You're lost!"

"We *said* you were stupid!" jeered another. "You lose! We win!"

Cackling with delighted laughter, the sprites jumped up, flapped their bat-like wings and flew away.

Lost!

"We've got to get back to the sanctuary
and help poor Winterberry!" cried
Summer.

"But how?" Jasmine asked helplessly.
She went to where the path had been,
still carrying the snow bear cub, but there
were tree trunks blocking the way now.
"The path's gone."

Summer swung round to Trixi. "Can
you help us, Trixi?"

"I'll try." Trixi thought for a minute. Then she tapped her pixie ring and chanted:

"Pixie magic, help us see.
Light the way to the sanctuary."

Her pixie ring glowed, and then the light faded. Trixi shook her head hopelessly.

"It's no good. Queen Malice's magic has blocked my spell. My pixie magic isn't strong enough to defeat her."

"We have to be able to find our way back somehow," said Jasmine. She put the snow bear down so she could think.

The others did the same. The cubs were very cute but they were quite heavy after a while! The cubs shook themselves and trotted around by the girls' feet, nosing at the snow and tree trunks.

Jasmine bit her lip and paced up and down. What could they do? They were deep in the forest now. If they set off into the trees and went the wrong way they could be lost for days!

One of the cubs ran over to Ellie and pawed at her leg. She could hear his tummy rumbling. He whimpered.

"I'm sorry, there isn't any food or milk out here," Ellie told him sadly. She crouched down and stroked his fur. "I'd love to get you home and give you some warm milk, but we're lost."

The bear cub looked at her for a
moment with puzzled dark eyes. Then
he made a little rumbling sound in his
throat and looked over at the trees before
looking back at her. Ellie frowned. It was
as if he was trying to tell her something.
She wished she had the magic unicorn
horn from the Magic Box that let them
talk to animals. "What are you trying to
tell me?" she whispered to him.

Suddenly the bear cub ran off towards
the trees. The other two cubs followed
him.

"Come back!" Summer cried anxiously.
"You'll get lost!" The cubs stopped by
the trees and looked round at them.
The one who had been with Ellie made
a hopeful whining noise and pawed at
the ground, staring up at her with his

chocolate-brown eyes. Ellie frowned.
Why was he looking at her like that?

Summer was close to tears. "There's
nothing we can do. This time Queen
Malice really has beaten us."

Jasmine put her arm round her. "Don't
say that."

"No, don't!" Ellie cried, staring at the bear cub as an idea popped into her head. "I think we can find our way back."

"How?" Jasmine, Summer and Trixi demanded.

Ellie pointed to the cubs. "By following the snow bears!" Her eyes shone. "I think they know the way to the sanctuary."

The cubs snuffled at the ground, ran a little way into the trees and then stopped as if waiting for the girls to follow them.

"Of course!" said Summer. "They'll be able to use their sense of smell to get back – it won't matter to them that the path has disappeared. All the bears go to the sanctuary when they're cold and hungry, just like the cubs are now!" She grabbed Jasmine and Ellie's hands.

"Come on! Let's follow them!"

The bears trotted on into the trees. The girls rushed after them with Trixi zooming alongside. It was harder running through trees and not following a path, but the girls refused to slow down. They had to get back to Snow Bear Sanctuary as quickly as possible!

The bears galloped on ahead.
Gradually the trees started to thin out
and the girls saw the lights of the cabin
up ahead through the tree trunks. "We're
almost there!" cried Ellie.

"I wonder what damage the ogre has
done?" Jasmine said anxiously.

They reached the end of the trees. With
dismay they saw that the cabin door had
been completely smashed down, and they
could hear bangs and crashes coming
from inside.

The cubs heard the noise and slowed to
a stop.

"Girls!" They all looked round.
Winterberry came hurrying out of the
trees just to their left. In the trees all
around her the girls could see the shapes
of the other bears that had been in the

house. "Oh, I'm so glad you're all safe!" Winterberry cried.

The cubs immediately galloped over to the brownie. She crouched down and hugged them. "And you three naughty cubs! I hoped you'd found the girls – I was so worried."

"What happened?" asked Ellie.

"The ogre came to the house and broke the door down. The bears and I got out through the back door and hid here," Winterberry said. "Luckily he hasn't started exploring the huts yet, he's just been in the house."

"Looks like we got back just in time then," said Jasmine, relieved that none of the other bears had been hurt. "Have you got the book, Trixi?"

"Yes." Trixi pulled it out and handed it to Jasmine. It was tiny on Jasmine's outstretched palm. Trixi tapped her pixie ring and a shower of sparks flew out and rained down over the book.

It immediately grew back to its normal size.

"That ogre had better say goodbye to the Secret Kingdom – he's going back where he belongs!" Jasmine said, turning the pages until she found the story with the ogre in. All the pictures in the third fairytale had an ogre-shaped space in them. If they could just get close to the ogre then the book's magic would suck him back into the pages. There was only one problem with that – how did they get close enough without being flattened by the ogre's club or becoming his lunchtime snack?

"Oh, do be careful!" Trixi cried.

"I'm really not sure you should go in there," said Winterberry anxiously.

"We have to!" Summer replied bravely.

The girls stepped towards the house.

"Wait! I'm coming with you," said Winterberry. "I can't let you go in alone. I'll just put the cubs in one of the sheds so they don't get into trouble. The older bears are sensible enough to stay out of the way. Come on, cubs, there's yummy bearberry jam this way!"

The cubs gambolled eagerly after her. Winterberry opened the door of the nearest hut and gently bundled them inside. Then she shut the door and pushed the bolt across. "Right, that should keep them safe," she said.

They all approached Winterberry's cabin cautiously. It had gone very quiet inside. What was the ogre doing? Maybe he had spotted them and was lying in wait...

They reached the door.

Jasmine took a deep breath. "All right, this is it!" she whispered to her friends. "We're going in!"

The Very
Hungry Ogre

The cabin door was hanging off its
hinges, the wood cracked and splintered.
Jasmine eased it open and the three girls
and Winterberry crept inside with Trixi
crouching on her leaf beside them.

They looked round the hall. Everything
was in complete chaos. There were
flowers on the floor, a vase was broken
and the lounge door had a massive hole

in it. All the furniture inside the cosy room had been smashed to smithereens. The girls gasped in horror. The little cottage had been ruined!

"Look at the mess!" Winterberry whispered in dismay. "He's destroyed everything."

"Where is he now?" hissed Ellie anxiously.

They all listened. There was just silence.

Jasmine noticed that the door to the kitchen was open and crept towards it.

"RRRRRRRRRRR!"

Everyone jumped as a deep sound rumbled out of the kitchen.

"That must be the ogre growling," whispered Ellie. Her mouth felt dry.

"He sounds v-very fierce," quavered

Trixi, trembling on her little leaf.

"RRRRRRRRRRRR!"

Summer frowned. There was something not quite right about the growl. There was a breathy catch at the start of it, almost as if the ogre was breathing in deeply, just like when the snow bear cubs had been asleep… Of course! "It's not a growl!" she said quickly. "It's a snore!"

Ellie and Jasmine looked at her curiously.

"You mean you think he's asleep?" asked Jasmine. She tiptoed to the door. Her eyes widened and she beckoned the others over.

The kitchen was a scene of devastation. Everything had been swept from the shelves and table onto the floor. Plates were smashed, pans lay on their side,

bags of flour and sugar had burst open.
And slumped on the floor, sleeping with
his head resting back against one of the
cupboards, was the massive ogre. Beside
him was a giant bowl of bearberry jam.
His cheeks were sticky and pink, just like
the cubs' had been in the forest.

"He's been eating the jam!" said Ellie in astonishment.

The ogre's eyelids flickered. "Me hungry," he muttered sadly. "Foooood!" He mumbled and brushed at his face before his eyes shut again and another long snore escaped him. "RRRRRRRRRRRR!"

"Oh, the poor thing," burst out kind-hearted Winterberry. "He's just hungry! He was looking for food."

At the sound of her voice the ogre's eyes opened once more. Although the rest of him was very ugly, Summer noticed that his eyes were soft and brown.

"People!" he said, sitting up.

"We're not food!" Ellie gasped.

The ogre blinked in astonishment.

"Trog no eat people. People yucky!"

"What about pixies?' Trixi quavered.

"Puh!" Trog wrinkled his nose. "Trog like jam. Jam and fruit and biscuits."

"Is Trog your name?" Jasmine said curiously.

The ogre nodded. "Trog look for food but when he ask bears in woods, they run away. Trog just want something to eat."

"Oh, you poor lamb," said Winterberry. She hurried over to the massive ogre and patted his arm. "You must be starving. Well, don't you worry, Trog. I'll sort you out with some food straight away. How about some lovely fresh cookies and bearberry juice, and then I can find some more bearberry jam for you to eat." She fussed over the ugly ogre as if he was one of her snow bears.

"You must be hungry as well," she said
to the girls. "And the cubs need their
milk and jam too."

"We can help feed them," said Jasmine.
"But let's get this place tidied up first."

"No need for you to do that!" Trixi
smiled. "You know my magic is great for
tidying up."

She tapped her ring and chanted,

"Pixie magic, mend and clean,
Make this little cabin gleam!"

A fountain of silver sparkles shot out of
the ring and spun round the cabin. The
girls watched in delight as everything
sorted itself out. The pots mended
themselves and jumped back onto the

shelves, the flour and sugar bags were refilled, the spilled food disappeared and the doors became whole again. Soon Winterberry's home was back to normal.

While the ogre ate his way through a huge plateful of cookies and jam, the girls helped Winterberry warm the bottles up for the snow bear cubs.

"Much better!" the ogre said. He patted his bulging tummy. "Trog full! Thank you, kind brownie." His eyes grew sad. "Trog misses his home. His warm sunny home where fruit grows on all the trees. Trog no want to be here in this cold place."

"Don't worry, Trog," said Jasmine. "We can help you get back to your proper home." She picked the book up from where she had left it on the side and opened it up. A bright golden light shone out, making Trog blink in surprise.

"The magic will take you home," said Ellie.

"I'm glad you were a nice ogre." Summer grinned.

"Nice people," said Trog with a smile. "Thank you!"

The golden light surrounded him and suddenly he disappeared. The light swirled back into the book and when the girls looked at the pages they saw Trog in the pictures again. He was back where he belonged!

"Wow," said Jasmine, breathing a sigh of relief. "I never imagined the ogre we were looking for was going to be nice."

"He was such a dear," agreed Winterberry. "I can't thank you enough for helping him get home, though. He really was upsetting my poor bears. Now he's gone, they'll all be able to go back to their homes in the forest."

"Talking of bears," said Summer, listening to the cubs whining outside, "I think the cubs want their milk."

Winterberry opened the cabin door and

the baby bears tumbled inside. The girls
took the bottles through and sat down on
the comfy sofas with the pink fluffy cubs.
They snuggled them down into their
arms and fed them the bottles of milk.

As the flames in the fireplace flickered, Winterberry brought them mugs of her delicious hot chocolate. Jasmine drank hers and sighed happily, resting her head against the back of the sofa. She felt her eyes closing. It had been another very exciting adventure!

"Wake up, Jasmine," Ellie giggled,

nudging her. "You can't fall asleep
here."

Jasmine blinked and woke up. "Sorry.
It's just so warm and comfy." She
yawned and stretched. The cubs were all
asleep on their laps.

Summer stroked the snoozing cub. "I
wish we didn't have to go home," she
said longingly, kissing his head.

"Remember, we're going back to see
lots of other animals at the zoo," Ellie
reminded her.

"And you are welcome to come back
and visit the snow bears whenever you
want to," said Winterberry. "I really
can't thank you enough for all you have
done. Now the snow bears can feel safe
again."

Summer felt much happier. "I'll see you

three soon," she whispered to the sleeping cubs as she and the others laid them gently together on the sofa in a fluffy, snoring pile.

Trixi tapped her ring. "I'll tell King Merry what happened here and see you all again when we find out where the next baddie is. Goodbye!"

"Bye!" the girls cried as a cloud of sparkling colours surrounded them and whisked them away.

They landed with a bump back on

the grass near the penguin pool at
Honeyvale Zoo. It was very strange
to be back in the bright sunshine, with
green grass all around them rather than
pink snow. The Magic Box was on the
ground between them and their clothes
were back to normal.

"What a brilliant adventure!' said Ellie.
"I loved the snow bears!"

"Me too," said Summer. She scooped

up the Magic Box and put it back in her bag. "And I never thought the ogre would turn out to be nice!"

"That's another baddie back in the book – just three to go," said Jasmine.

"I wonder how scary the next one will be?" Summer said.

"However scary it is, we'll capture it and send it back where it belongs!" declared Jasmine. "We're going to make the Secret Kingdom safe for everyone again."

"Girls!" They heard Jasmine's mum calling them and they came out from behind the sign. Mrs Smith waved. "The penguins are going to be fed in a few minutes!"

"Ooh! Come on!" said Summer.

Ellie grinned. "What's a penguin's

favourite food?"

"What?" said Jasmine.

"Iceberg lettuce, of course!" Ellie joked.

Summer and Jasmine snorted with laughter as they held hands and ran across the grass to the penguin enclosure.

In the next Secret Kingdom
adventure, Ellie, Summer and
Jasmine visit

Phoenix Festival

Read on for a sneak peek...

A Mysterious
Light

"I don't think I could be wearing any
more clothes!" Jasmine Smith giggled
to her best friends, Ellie Macdonald
and Summer Hammond. "I can hardly
walk!" She was dressed in a jumper,
jeans and wellies, plus a thick coat, a
scarf and some woolly mittens, and she
had a pair of pink furry earmuffs plonked

over her long dark hair.

"Same here," laughed Ellie, who had a pom-pom hat, scarf and gloves on top of her other clothes. "I'm wearing two vests and a pair of woolly tights under my trousers. And I still feel cold!"

It was fireworks night and the three friends were out on Honeyvale Hill with their families, waiting for the display to begin. It seemed like the whole village was there too, with everyone wrapped up cosily, tucking into hot dogs and toffee apples. Summer sniffed the cold air, recognising the scent of wood smoke from the bonfire. The golden flames rose into the night, twisting and flickering. It looks almost magical, she thought.

"Anybody want a sparkler?" Ellie's dad asked, coming over with a packet.

"Yes please!" cried Ellie.

"Me too!" said Summer.

"Me three!" laughed Jasmine.

Ellie's dad handed them each a sparkler. "Remember to hold them carefully, girls," he said as he carefully lit them and they burst into bright silver sparkles. "There's a bucket of water over by the hot dog stand, so once your sparkler burns out drop it in the water to let it cool down."

Mr Macdonald went off to light another sparkler for Molly, Ellie's little sister, leaving the three friends to wave theirs, creating fizzing patterns of light in the darkness.

Summer wrote her name with hers, loving the way it sputtered and sparked. Ellie drew wild, swirling patterns in the air, like a gigantic scribble. And Jasmine made zigzaggy lines of light that seemed to hang in the dark sky for a second before fading.

"The sparkles remind me of Trixi's pixie magic," Summer said dreamily.

"There's always that bright flash of light when she taps her ring to cast a spell."

"You're right," Ellie replied, smiling to herself as she thought about Trixi. She was one of their friends from the Secret Kingdom – a royal pixie who helped King Merry, the ruler there. The girls had discovered the Secret Kingdom by chance when they found a small wooden box at their school jumble sale. They hadn't known then that the box would lead them into lots of adventures in a magical land!

Once their sparklers had burned out, the girls dropped them into the bucket of water with a sizzle and a splash. Then they each got a hot dog – Jasmine added lots of fried onions to hers, Ellie squirted on a thick line of tomato ketchup and

Summer kept hers plain.

They were just thinking about what to do next when a voice called out to them. "Oh, there you are, girls!" Mrs Hammond, Summer's mum, came over, holding hands with Finn and Connor, Summer's little brothers. "Summer, love, I think you've left your bedroom light on, look."

Summer and her friends turned to see where her mum was pointing. Summer's house faced Honeyvale Hill but it was hard to make out exactly where it was in the velvety darkness.

Then Summer noticed that one house had a single lit window upstairs. Oh dear – that was her bedroom, she could see her row of fluffy bears on the windowsill. "Sorry, Mum," she said. A frown creased her forehead. "I'm sure I turned it off though," she murmured. Jasmine and Ellie had stayed for tea after school that afternoon, and they'd got changed up there together. In fact, now that she thought about it, she could actually remember flicking off the light switch as they came out because they'd been plunged into darkness for a moment. Jasmine had given a pretend scream and Summer had laughed as she fumbled to find the light.

"Never mind," her mum said. "Try to remember next time. Are you all having fun?"

"Mmmm," Summer said, only half-listening. She glanced back across at her lit bedroom, feeling confused…and then a shiver of excitement went through her.

Could it be the light from the Magic Box that was shining up there?

"Er…Actually, we should probably go back and turn it off," she said quickly. "It's bad to waste electricity. Mrs Taylor's always saying so at school. And it'll only take a minute."

Finn stamped his foot. "I don't WANT to go back," he grumbled. "I want a hot dog!"

"Well, us three can go, Mum, if you give me the key," Summer suggested. "I promise I won't lose it. We'll just go straight there and come back." She could see Ellie and Jasmine giving her puzzled looks, but knew she couldn't possibly start talking about the Magic Box in front of her mum. The three friends were the only ones who knew about their

magic adventures, and they wanted it to
stay that way!

Mrs Hammond looked surprised too.
"Don't worry," she said. "There's no
need—"

"It'll only take a minute," Summer
said. "Please? Anyway, I need the loo."
She crossed her fingers behind her back.
It wasn't strictly true about needing the
loo, but she was desperate to go back to
her bedroom and investigate.

If the Magic Box was calling her, Ellie and Jasmine, they needed to be there!

"Oh, all right," Mrs Hammond said as Finn and Connor began trying to drag her away to the hot dog stand. She let go of their hands for a moment to reach in her bag and find the key. "Take my torch as well," she said, passing it to Summer. "And come straight back, okay? No messing about."

"We will, I promise," Summer replied. "Thanks, Mum. We won't be long."

As Mrs Hammond and the boys walked off, Jasmine and Ellie both looked at Summer curiously. "What was all that about?" Jasmine asked.

Summer grinned and pointed at her bedroom. "I know I turned the light off in there," she said, walking briskly across the field. "So the light we can see shining can only be from—"

"The Magic Box!" Ellie realised, breaking into a run. "Come on! What are we waiting for? Trixi needs us!"

An Exciting Invitation

Whenever there was trouble in the Secret Kingdom, Trixi used the Magic Box to send for the only people who could help – Summer, Ellie and Jasmine! All the problems in the wonderful land were caused by mean Queen Malice, King Merry's horrible sister, who was angry that the people had chosen her kindly brother as their leader instead of her.

Recently Queen Malice had unleashed a collection of nasty characters from Summer's fairytale book into the kingdom, hoping they'd cause so many problems that everyone would beg her to rule just to make them go away. But Trixi and the girls were determined not to let that happen!

"I wonder if a new fairytale baddie has appeared," Summer said anxiously as they hurried across the field. "I hope it isn't a really scary one."

"At least the ogre wasn't too horrible," Jasmine said, remembering the last baddie they'd put back in the book. He had actually turned out to be quite nice, but they'd also helped Trixi and King Merry defeat a mean giant and a wicked witch – and those two definitely hadn't been nice at all!

Read

Phoenix Festival

to find out what
happens next!

Have you read all the books in Series 3?

Enjoy six sparkling adventures!

Be in on the secret.
Collect them all!

Enchanted Palace
ROSIE BANKS

Unicorn Valley
ROSIE BANKS

Cloud Island
ROSIE BANKS

Mermaid Reef
ROSIE BANKS

Magic Mountain
ROSIE BANKS

Glitter Beach
ROSIE BANKS

Series 1

When Jasmine, Summer and Ellie discover
the magical land of the Secret Kingdom,
a whole world of adventure awaits!

Secret Kingdom

Series 2

Wicked Queen Malice has cast a spell to turn King Merry into a toad! Can the girls find six magic ingredients to save him?

Look out for the next sparkling series!

In Series 4,
meet the magical Animal Keepers of the
Secret Kingdom, who spread fun, friendship,
kindness and bravery throughout the land!

When wicked Queen Malice casts an evil spell
to reverse the Keepers' powers, it's up to Ellie,
Summer and Jasmine to find each animal's
magical charm and reunite them with their
Keeper – before their special values disappear
from the kingdom forever!

Available
February 2014

In **Glitter Bird**, Ellie, Summer and Jasmine must reunite the Bird Keeper with his magical charm to make the Secret Kingdom fun again!

Can you find a way through the maze to reach the bird? Watch out for Storm Sprites!

Secret Kingdom

Competition!

Evil Queen Malice has been up to no good again and hidden six of her naughty Storm Sprites in the pages of each Secret Kingdom book in series three!

Did you spot the Storm Sprite while you were reading this book?

Ellie, Summer and Jasmine need your help!

Can you find the pages where the cheeky Sprites are hiding in each of the six books in series three?

When you have found all six Storm Sprites, go online and tell us what pages they are hiding on and enter the competition at

www.secretkingdombooks.com

We will put all of the correct entries into a draw and select one winner to receive a special Secret Kingdom goodie bag featuring lots of sparkly gifts, including a glittery t-shirt!

Collect the tokens from each Secret Kingdom book to get special Secret Kingdom gifts!

In every Secret Kingdom book there are three Friendship Tokens that you can exchange for special gifts! Save up all the tokens from the back of the books. Once you've collected 18, send them in to us to get a bumper goodie bag of activities and gifts!

Surprise goodies inside!

To take part in this offer, please send us a letter telling us why you like Secret Kingdom books so much! Don't forget to:

1) Include your name and address
2) Include the signature of a parent or guardian

Send your tokens to:
Secret Kingdom Friendship Token Offer
Orchard Books Marketing Department
338 Euston Road, London, NW1 3BH

Closing date: 29th November 2013

www.secretkingdombooks.com

1 Friendship Token	1 Friendship Token	1 Friendship Token
www.secretkingdombooks.com	www.secretkingdombooks.com	www.secretkingdombooks.com
Secret Kingdom	Secret Kingdom	Secret Kingdom

Secret Kingdom

A magical world of friendship and fun!

Join best friends Ellie, Summer and Jasmine at

www.secretkingdombooks.com

and enjoy games, sneak peeks and lots more!

You'll find great activities, competitions, stories
and games, plus a special newsletter for
Secret Kingdom friends!